Due

BLY Jul 9

OCT - 5 1

MAY 24 1

MAR - 4 1

MAR 2 8

AUG 3

DEC 1

JUL

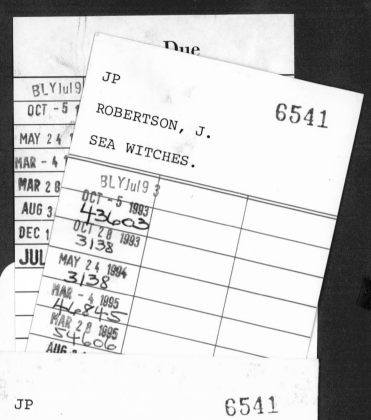

JP   6541

ROBERTSON, J.

SEA WITCHES.

BLY Jul 9 3		
OCT - 5 1993 43603		
OCT 2 8 1993 3138		
MAY 24 1994 3138		
MAR - 4 1995 4845		
MAR 2 8 1995 5606		
AUG 3		

JP   6541

ROBERTSON, J.

SEA WITCHES.

SEA WITCHES

SEA WITCHES

by
Joanne Robertson

illustrated by
Laszlo Gal

TORONTO OXFORD NEW YORK
OXFORD UNIVERSITY PRESS
1991

Oxford University Press, 70 Wynford Drive, Don Mills, Ontario, M3C 1J9

Toronto   Oxford   New York   Delhi   Bombay   Calcutta   Madras   Karachi
Petaling Jaya   Singapore   Hong Kong   Tokyo   Nairobi   Dar es Salaam
Cape Town   Melbourne   Auckland

and associated companies in
Berlin   Ibadan

Canadian Cataloguing in Publication Data
Robertson, Joanne, 1946 –
Sea Witches
ISBN 0-19-540800-4
I. Gal, Laszlo. II. Title.
PS8585.024S4 1991   jC811'.54   C90-094029-8
PZ8.3.R6Se 1991

1 2 3 4 – 4 3 2 1

Printed in Hong Kong

To Richard, with love.
—J.R.

To Bill Toye,
my first Canadian publisher.
—L.G.

With this weird warning
My Scottish grandmother served
Soft-boiled eggs for lunch:

"When you're done eating,
Give your eggshells a beating!
Never leave them whole!"

"Why?" I would ask her,
While into sharp jagged shards
I shattered the shells.

This story she told:
"Ghastly ghost witches gather
In the darkling gloom.

Silently they come,
Broom-riding, hideous hags,
In search of eggshells.

Down to earth they steal,
Weaving eerie, evil spells
And gathering shells.

Hocus, Pocus, Pow!
Waving wands and witches' words
Work their magic now.

Shells turn into ships,
Delicate eggshell vessels,
Wretched roundabouts.

Hidden by the mist,
Seaworthy and watertight,
They head out to sea:

Wandering witches
Search the sea for sailing ships
Of honest seamen.

A ship heaves in sight!
Ahoy! On the horizon!
Unsuspecting prey.

Witches wail and howl,
Hidden in a thundercloud,
Stirring up the seas.

Whistling up the wind,
Whipping and whirling it 'round,
They gather power.

A black cloud, white edged,
Churning troubled waters white,
Gives sailors warning.

The witch-storm attacks —
Savage winds and lashing rain
From lightning-streaked clouds.

Blackened brutal seas,
Battering the bruised vessel,
Boil furiously.

Witches raise a wall
of water before the ship –
Steel sky, iron sea.

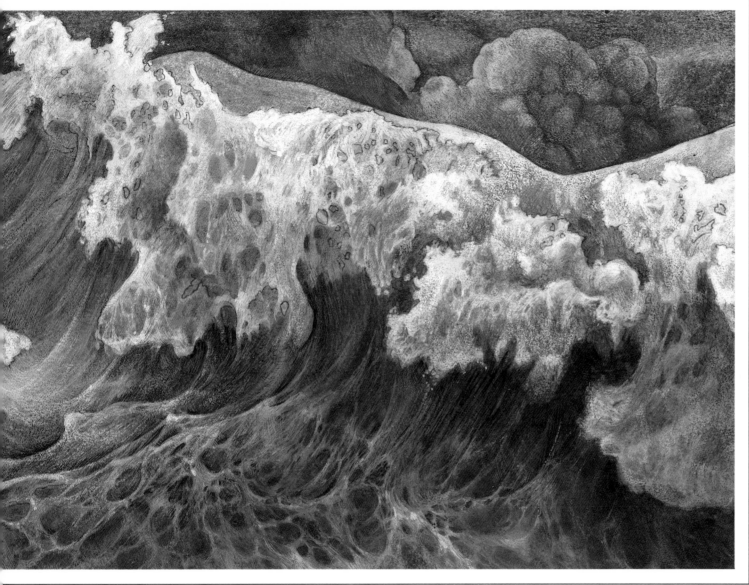

Destroying the ship,
Raging, unyielding waters
Swallow the seamen.

The drowned ship goes down
The long throat of the ocean
To cavernous depths.

Whooping and cheering,
Victorious witches watch
The watery wreck.

Escaping on brooms,
Sea witches cackle and shriek,
Their wicked work done.

Powdery remains
Of abandoned eggshell ships
Are left in their wake.

Undersea sailors,
Deep in Davey Jones' Locker
Can never go home.

Rocked in water beds,
They sleep on seashell pillows,
Dreaming of beaches."

The story's over.
But be sure to remember
Grandmother's warning:

"When you're done eating,
Give your eggshells a beating!
Never leave them whole!"

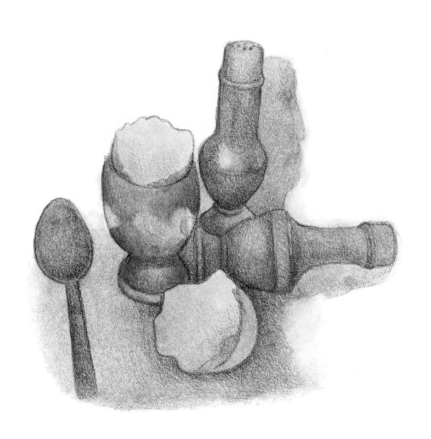